BADGER

TOAD HALL

MOLE

This edition published exclusively
for Marks and Spencer p.l.c.
by Purnell Books, member of the BPCC Group,
Paulton, Bristol BS18 5LQ
Fifth impression

ISBN 0 361 06008 4
Copyright © 1983 Purnell Publishers Limited
Published August 1983
Made and printed in Great Britain by Purnell and Sons
(Book Production) Limited, Paulton, Bristol

# Tales from
# THE WIND IN THE WILLOWS

## KENNETH GRAHAME

Abridged for younger readers

## Illustrations by Val Biro

*St Michael*

# The River Bank

The Mole had been working very hard all the morning, spring-cleaning his little home. Suddenly he flung down his brush on the floor, said "Bother!" and "O blow!" and also "Hang spring-cleaning!" and bolted out of the house without even waiting to put on his coat.

The sunshine struck hot on his fur and he thought his happiness was complete when, as he meandered aimlessly along, suddenly he stood by the edge of a full-fed river. Never in his life had he seen a river before.

"Hullo, Mole!" said a Water Rat on the opposite bank.

"Hullo, Rat!" said the Mole.

"Would you like to come over?" inquired the Rat presently.

"O, it's all very well to *talk*," said the Mole.

The Rat said nothing, but stooped and unfastened a rope and hauled on it; then lightly stepped into a little boat. He sculled smartly across and made fast. Then he held up his fore-paw as the Mole stepped gingerly down. "Lean on that!" he said. "Now then, step lively!" and the Mole to his surprise and rapture found himself actually seated in the stern of a real boat.

"This is a wonderful day!" said he, as the Rat shoved off and took to the sculls again. "Do you know, I've never been in a boat before in all my life."

"What?" cried the Rat, open-mouthed. "Never been in a—you never—well, I—what have you been doing, then?"

"Is it so nice as all that?" asked the Mole shyly.

"Nice? It's the *only* thing," said the Water Rat solemnly, as he leant forward for his stroke. "Believe me, my young friend, there is *nothing*—absolutely nothing—half so much worth doing as simply messing about in boats. Look here! If you've nothing else on hand this morning, supposing we drop down the river together, and have a long day of it?"

The Mole waggled his toes from sheer happiness. "*What* a day I'm having!" he said. "Let us start at once!"

"Hold hard a minute, then!" said the Rat. He looped the painter through a ring in his landing-stage, climbed up into his hole above, and after a short time reappeared staggering under a fat, wicker luncheon-basket.

"Shove that under your feet," he observed to the Mole, as he passed it down into the boat.

"What's inside it?" asked the Mole.

"There's cold chicken inside it," replied the Rat briefly; "coldtonguecoldhamcoldbeefpickledgherkinssaladfrenchrollscress sandwidgespottedmeatgingerbeerlemonadesodawater—"

"O stop, stop," cried the Mole in ecstasies: "This is too much!"

The Mole, spellbound by the sparkle, the ripple, the scents and the sounds and the sunlight, trailed a paw in the water and dreamed long waking dreams. The Water Rat, like the good little fellow he was, sculled steadily on and did not disturb him.

"What lies over *there*?" asked the Mole, waving a paw towards a background of woodland that darkly framed the water-meadows on one side of the river.

"That? O, that's just the Wild Wood," said the Rat shortly. "We don't go there very much, we river-bankers."

"Aren't they—aren't they very *nice* people in there?" said the Mole a trifle nervously.

"W-e-ll," replied the Rat, "You can't really trust them, and that's a fact."

The Mole knew well that it is quite against animal-etiquette to dwell on possible trouble ahead, so he dropped the subject.

"Now then!" said the Rat, "Here's our backwater at last, where we're going to lunch."

He brought the boat alongside the bank, made her fast, helped the still awkward Mole safely ashore, and swung out the luncheon-basket. The Mole begged as a favour to be allowed to unpack it all by himself; and the Rat was pleased to indulge him.

When all was ready, the Rat said: "Now, pitch in, old fellow!" and the Mole was indeed very glad to obey, for he had started his spring-cleaning at a very early hour that morning.

Just then a broad glistening muzzle showed itself above the edge of the bank, and the Otter hauled himself out and shook the water from his coat.

"Greedy beggars!" he observed, making for the food. "Why didn't you invite me, Ratty?"

"This was an impromptu affair," explained the Rat. "By the way—my friend, Mr Mole."

"Proud, I'm sure," said the Otter.

There was a rustle behind them, proceeding from a hedge wherein last year's leaves still clung thick, and a stripy head, with high shoulders behind it, peered forth on them.

"Come on, old Badger!" shouted the Rat.

The Badger trotted forward a pace or two; then grunted, "H'm! Company," and turned his back and disappeared from view.

"That's *just* the sort of fellow he is!" observed the disappointed Rat. "Simply hates Society! Now we shan't see any more of him today. Well, tell us *who's* out on the river?"

"Toad's out, for one," replied the Otter. "In his brand-new boat; new togs, new everything!"

The two animals looked at each other and laughed.

"Once, it was nothing but sailing," said the Rat. "Then he tired of that and took to punting. It's all the same, whatever he takes up; he gets tired of it, and starts on something fresh."

"Such a good fellow, too," remarked the Otter. "But no stability—especially in a boat!"

An errant May-fly swerved unsteadily by. A swirl of water and a 'cloop!' and the May-fly was visible no more.

Neither was the Otter.

The Rat hummed a tune, and the Mole recollected that animal-etiquette forbade any sort of comment on the sudden disappearance of one's friends at any moment, for any reason or no reason whatever.

"Well, well," said the Rat, "I suppose we ought to be moving."

The afternoon sun was getting low as the Rat sculled gently homewards in a dreamy mood, murmuring poetry-things over to himself, and not paying much attention to Mole. But the Mole was getting a bit restless: and presently he said, "Ratty! Please, *I* want to row, now!"

The Rat shook his head with a smile. "Not yet, my young friend," he said—"wait till you've had a few lessons. It's not so

easy as it looks."

The Mole jumped up and seized the sculls, so suddenly, that the Rat was taken by surprise and fell backwards off his seat.

Over went the boat, and the Mole found himself struggling in the river. Then a firm paw gripped him by the back of his neck. It was the Rat, and he was evidently laughing—the Mole could *feel* him laughing, right down his arm and through his paw, and so into his—the Mole's—neck.

The Rat steered the helpless animal to shore, hauled him out and set him down on the bank.

When all was ready for a start once more, the Mole, limp and dejected, took his seat in the stern of the boat; and as they set off, he said in a low voice, broken with emotion, "Ratty, my generous friend! I am very sorry indeed for my foolish and ungrateful conduct."

"That's all right, bless you!" responded the Rat cheerily. "What's a little wet to a Water Rat? I'm more in the water than out of it most days. Don't you think any more about it; and, look here! I really think you had better come and stop with me for a little time. I'll teach you to row, and to swim, and you'll soon be as handy on the water as any of us."

This day was only the first of many similar ones for the Mole, each of them longer and fuller of interest as the ripening summer moved onward. He learnt to swim and to row, and entered into the joy of running water; and with his ear to the reed-stems he caught, at intervals, something of what the wind went whispering so constantly among them.

# The Open Road

"Ratty," said the Mole suddenly, one bright summer morning, "Won't you take me to call on Mr Toad? I've heard so much about him, and I do so want to make his acquaintance."

"Why, certainly," said the good-natured Rat. "Get the boat out, and we'll paddle up there at once.

Rounding a bend in the river, they came in sight of a handsome, dignified old house of mellowed red brick, with well-kept lawns reaching down to the water's edge.

"There's Toad Hall," said the Rat; "and that creek on the left, where the notice-board says *Private. No landing allowed,* leads to his boat-house, where we'll leave the boat. Toad is rather rich, you know, and this is really one of the nicest houses in these parts, though we never admit as much to Toad."

They disembarked, and strolled across the gay flower-decked lawns in search of Toad, whom they presently happened upon resting in a wicker garden-chair, with a preoccupied expression of face, and a large map spread out on his knees.

"Hooray!" he cried, jumping up on seeing them, "this is splendid!" He shook the paws of both of them warmly, never waiting for an introduction to the Mole. "How *kind* of you!" he went on, dancing round them. "I was just going to send a boat down the river for you, Ratty, with strict orders that you were to be fetched up here at once, whatever you were doing. I want you badly—both of you. Now what will you take? Come inside and have something! You don't know how lucky it is, your turning up just now!"

"It's about your rowing, I suppose," said the Rat.

"O, pooh! boating!" interrupted the Toad, in great disgust. "Silly boyish amusement. I've given that up *long* ago. Come with me, dear Ratty, and your amiable friend also, if he will be so very good, just as far as the stable-yard!"

He led the way to the stable-yard accordingly, and there they saw a gipsy caravan, shining with newness, painted a canary-yellow picked out with green, and red wheels.

"There you are!" cried the Toad. "There's real life for you, embodied in that little cart. The open road, the dusty highway! Here today, up and off to somewhere else tomorrow!"

The Mole was tremendously interested and excited, and followed him eagerly up the steps and into the interior of the caravan. The Rat only snorted and thrust his hands deep into his pockets, remaining where he was.

"All complete!" said the Toad triumphantly. "You'll find that nothing whatever has been forgotten, when we make our start this afternoon."

"I beg your pardon," said the Rat slowly, as he chewed a straw, "but did I overhear you say something about "*we*", and "*start*", and "*this afternoon*"?"

"Now, you dear good old Ratty," said Toad imploringly, "don't begin talking in that stiff and sniffy sort of way, because you know you've *got* to come."

"I don't care," said the Rat doggedly. "I'm not coming, and that's flat. And what's more, Mole's going to stick to me and do as I do, aren't you, Mole?"

"Of course I am," said the Mole loyally. "I'll always stick to you, Rat, and what you say is to be—has got to be. All the same, it sounds as if it might have been—well, rather fun, you know!" he added wistfully.

The Rat saw what was passing in his mind, and wavered. Toad was watching both of them closely.

"Come along in and have some lunch," he said diplomatically, "and we'll talk it over." During luncheon it soon seemed taken for granted by all three of them that the trip was a settled thing.

When they were quite ready, the now triumphant Toad led his companions to the paddock and set them to capture the old grey horse. Meantime Toad packed the lockers still tighter with necessaries, and hung nose-bags, nets of onions, bundles of hay, and baskets from the bottom of the cart. At last they were ready to start. They set off. It was a golden afternoon.

They were strolling along the high road easily, when far behind them they heard a faint warning hum, like the drone of a distant bee. Glancing back, they saw a small cloud of dust, with a dark centre of energy, advancing on them at incredible speed, while from out of the dust a faint 'Poop-poop!' wailed like an uneasy animal in pain. Hardly regarding it, they turned to resume their conversation, when in an instant (as it seemed) the peaceful scene was changed, and with a blast of wind and a whirl of sound that

made them jump for the nearest ditch, it was on them! The 'poop-poop' rang with a brazen shout in their ears and then the magnificent motor-car overtook them and dwindled to a speck in the far distance.

Rearing, plunging, backing steadily, the old horse drove the cart backwards towards the deep ditch at the side of the road. It wavered an instant—then there was a heartrending crash—and the canary-coloured cart, their pride and their joy, lay on its side in the ditch, an irredeemable wreck.

The Rat danced up and down in the road, simply transported with passion. "You villains!" he shouted, shaking both fists, "You scoundrels, you highwaymen, you—you road-hogs!—I'll have the law on you!"

Toad sat straight down in the middle of the dusty road, his legs stretched out before him, and stared fixedly in the direction of the disappearing motor-car.

"Glorious, stirring sight!" murmured Toad, never offering to move. "The *only* way to travel! Here today—in next week tomorrow! O bliss! O poop-poop! O my! O my!"

"What are we to do with him?" asked the Mole.

"Nothing at all," replied the Rat firmly. "Because there is really nothing to be done. You see, I know him from of old. He is now possessed. Never mind him. Let's go and see what there is to be done about the cart."

A careful inspection showed them that, even if they succeeded in righting it by themselves, the cart would travel no longer. The axles were in a hopeless state, and the missing wheel was shattered.

The Rat knotted the horse's reins over his back and took him by the head, carrying the bird-cage and its hysterical occupant in the other hand. "Come on!" he said grimly to the Mole. "It's five or six miles to the nearest town, and we shall just have to walk it. The sooner we make a start the better."

On reaching the town they went straight to the station and deposited Toad in the second-class waiting-room, giving a porter twopence to keep a strict eye on him. They then left the horse at an inn stable, and gave what directions they could about the cart and its contents. Eventually, a slow train having landed them at a station not very far from Toad Hall, they escorted the spellbound, sleep-walking Toad to his door, put him inside it, and instructed his housekeeper to feed him, undress him, and put him to bed. Then they sculled down the river home.

The following evening the Mole, who had risen late and taken things very easy all day, was sitting on the bank fishing, when the Rat, who had been looking up his friends and gossiping, came strolling along to find him. "Heard the news?" he said. "There's nothing else being talked about, all along the river bank. Toad went up to Town by an early train this morning. And he has ordered a large and very expensive motor-car."

# The Wild Wood

The Mole had long wanted to make the acquaintance of the Badger. But whenever the Mole mentioned his wish to the Water Rat he always found himself put off.

In the winter time the Rat slept a great deal, and so one afternoon, when the Rat was dozing in his arm-chair the Mole slipped out of the warm parlour into the open air. He pushed on towards the Wild Wood, which lay before him low and threatening, like a black reef in some still, southern sea.

There was nothing to alarm him at first entry. Twigs crackled under his feet, logs tripped him, funguses on stumps resembled caricatures, and startled him for the moment by their likeness to something familiar; but that was all fun, and exciting.

Then the faces began.

It was over his shoulder, and indistinctly, that he first thought he saw a face: a little evil wedge-shaped face, looking out at him from a hole. When he turned and confronted it, the thing had vanished.

If he could only get away from the holes in the banks, he thought, there would be no more faces. He swung off the path and plunged into the untrodden places of the wood.

Then the pattering began.

He thought it was only falling leaves at first, so slight and delicate was the sound of it. Then as it grew it took a regular rhythm, and he knew it for nothing else but the pat-pat-pat of little feet. In panic, he began to run too, aimlessly, he knew not whither. At last he took refuge in the dark deep hollow of an old beech tree. And as he lay there panting and trembling, he knew at last, in all its fullness, that which the Rat had vainly tried to shield him from—the Terror of the Wild Wood!

Meantime the Rat woke to find Mole gone. He left the house and carefully examined the muddy surface of the ground outside, hoping to find the Mole's tracks. He could see the imprints of them in the mud, running along straight and purposeful, leading directly to the Wild Wood.

The Rat looked very grave, and stood in deep thought for a minute or two. The he re-entered the house, strapped a belt round his waist, shoved a brace of pistols into it, took up a stout cudgel that stood in a corner of the hall, and set off for the Wild Wood at a smart pace all the time calling out cheerfully, "Moly, Moly, Moly! Where are you? It's me—it's old Rat!"

He had patiently hunted through the wood for an hour or more, when at last to his joy he heard a feeble voice saying, "Ratty! Is that really you?"

The Rat crept into the hollow, and there he found the Mole,

exhausted and still trembling. "O, Rat!" he cried, "I've been so frightened, you can't think!"

"O, I quite understand," said the Rat soothingly. "You shouldn't really have gone and done it, Mole. I did my best to keep you from it. Now we really must make a start for home while there's still a little light left."

"Dear Ratty," said the poor Mole, "I'm dreadfully sorry, but I'm simply dead beat and that's a solid fact. You *must* let me rest here a while and get my strength back, if I'm to get home at all."

When at last the Mole woke up, they found that it had been snowing hard.

"Well, well, it can't be helped," said the Rat after pondering.

"We must make a start, and take our chance, I suppose. The worst of it is, I don't exactly know where we are. And now this snow makes everything look so very different."

It did indeed. The Mole would not have known that it was the same wood. An hour or two later—they had lost all count of time—they pulled up, dispirited, weary, and hopelessly at sea, and sat down on a fallen tree-trunk to recover their breath and consider what was to be done. They were aching with fatigue and bruised with tumbles; they had fallen into several holes and got wet through; the snow was getting so deep that they could hardly

drag their little legs through it, and the trees were thicker and
more like each other than ever. There seemed to be no end to this
wood, and no beginning, and no difference in it, and, worst of all,
no way out.

Suddenly the Rat cried "Hooray!" and then "Hooray-ooray-oo-
ray-ooray!" and fell to executing a feeble jig in the snow.

"What *have* you found, Ratty?" asked the Mole.

"Come and see!" said the delighted Rat, as he jigged on.

The Mole hobbled up to the spot and had a good look.

"Well," he said at last, slowly, "I *see* it right enough. Seen the same sort of thing before, lots of times. A door-scraper! Well, what of it? Why dance jigs round a door-scraper?"

"Now look here, you—you thick-headed beast," replied the Rat, really angry, "scrape and scratch and dig and hunt round, especially on the sides of the hummocks, if you want to sleep dry and warm tonight, for it's our last chance!"

The Rat attacked a snow-bank beside them with ardour, probing with his cudgel everywhere and then digging with fury; and the Mole scraped busily too. Hard at it went the two animals, till at last the result of their labours stood full in view of the astonished and hitherto incredulous Mole.

In the side of what had seemed to be a snow-bank stood a solid-looking little door, painted a dark green. An iron bell-pull hung by the side, and below it, on a small brass plate, neatly engraved in square capital letters, they could read by the aid of moonlight:

While the Rat attacked the door with his stick, the Mole sprang up at the bell-pull, clutched it and swung there, both feet well off the ground, and from quite a long way off they could faintly hear a deep-toned bell respond.

# Mr Badger

They waited patiently for what seemed a very long time, stamping in the snow to keep their feet warm. At last there was the noise of a bolt shot back, and the door opened a few inches, enough to show a long snout and a pair of blinking eyes.

"O, Badger," cried the Rat, "let us in, please. It's me, Rat, and my friend Mole, and we've lost our way in the snow."

"What, Ratty, my dear little man!" exclaimed the Badger, in a most surprised voice. "Come along in, both of you, at once. Why, you must be perished. Well I never! Lost in the snow! And in the Wild Wood too, and at this time of night! But come in."

The two animals tumbled over each other in their eagerness to get inside, and heard the door shut behind them with great relief.

The Badger looked kindly down on them and patted both their heads. "This is not the sort of night for small animals to be out," he said paternally. "I'm afraid you've been up to some of your pranks again, Ratty. But come along; come into the kitchen. There's a first-rate fire there, and supper and everything."

When supper was really finished at last, the Badger said heartily, "Now then! tell us the news from your part of the world. How's old Toad going on?"

"O, from the bad to worse," said the Rat gravely, while the Mole, cocked up on a settle and basking in the firelight, his heels higher than his head, tried to look properly mournful. "Another smash-up in his car only last week, and a bad one. He's a hopelessly bad driver, and quite regardless of law and order. Killed or ruined—it's got to be one of the two things, sooner or later. Badger! we're his friends, oughtn't we to do something?"

"Very well then!" nodded the Badger. "*But*, when once the year has really turned, and the nights are shorter, and half-way through them one rouses and feels fidgety and wanting to be up and doing by sunrise, if not before—*you* know—!"

Both animals nodded gravely. *They* knew!

"Well, it's time we were all in bed," said the Badger, getting up and fetching flat candlesticks. "Come along, you two, and I'll show you your quarters. And take your time tomorrow morning—breakfast at any hour you please!"

In accordance with the kindly Badger's instructions, the two tired animals came down to breakfast very late next morning, and found a bright fire burning in the kitchen.

The Mole found himself placed next to Mr Badger, and took the opportunity to tell Badger how comfortable and home-like it all felt to him. "Once well underground," he said, "you know exactly where you are. Nothing can happen to you, and nothing can get at you. When you want to, up you go, and there the things are, waiting for you."

The Badger simply beamed on him. "That's exactly what I say," he replied. "There's no security, or peace and tranquillity, except underground."

The Mole assented heartily; and the Badger in consequence got very friendly with him.

The Rat began walking up and down, very restless. The underground atmosphere was getting on his nerves.

"Come along, Mole," he said anxiously. "We must get off while it's daylight. Don't want to spend another night in the Wild Wood."

"You really needn't fret, Ratty," said the Badger placidly. "My passages run further than you think, and I've bolt-holes to the edge of the wood in several directions, though I don't care for everybody to know about them. When you really have go, you shall leave by one of my short cuts. Meantime, make yourself easy, and sit down again."

The Rat was nevertheless still anxious to be off and attend to his river, so the Badger, taking up his lantern again, led the way

along a damp and airless tunnel that wound and dipped, part vaulted, part hewn through solid rock, for a weary distance that seemed to be miles. At last daylight began to show itself confusedly through tangled growth overhanging the mouth of the passage; and the Badger, bidding them a hasty good-bye, pushed them hurriedly through the opening, made everything look as natural as possible again, with creepers, brushwood, and dead leaves, and retreated.

They found themselves standing on the very edge of the Wild Wood; rocks and brambles and tree-roots behind them, confusedly heaped and tangled; in front, a great space of quiet fields, hemmed by lines of hedges black on the snow and, far ahead, a glint of the familiar old river, while the wintry sun hung red and low on the horizon.

Looking back, they saw the whole mass of the Wild Wood, dense, menacing, compact. Together they turned and made swiftly for home, for firelight and the familiar things it played on, for the voice, sounding cheerily outside their window, of the river that they knew and trusted, that never made them afraid.

# Mr Toad

It was a bright morning in the early part of summer. The Mole and the Water Rat had been up since dawn, very busy on matters connected with boats and the opening of the boating season. They were finishing breakfast in their little parlour and eagerly discussing their plans for the day, when a heavy knock sounded at the door.

"Bother!" said the Rat, all over egg. "See who it is, Mole, like a good chap, since you've finished."

The Mole went to attend the summons, and the Rat heard him utter a cry of surprise. Then he flung the parlour door open, and announced with much importance, "Mr Badger!"

The Badger strode heavily into the room.

"This very morning," began Badger, taking an arm-chair, "as I learnt last night from a trustworthy source, a new and exceptionally powerful motor-car will arrive at Toad Hall. You two animals will accompany me instantly to Toad Hall, and the work of rescue shall be accomplished."

"Right you are!" cried the Rat, starting up. "We'll rescue the poor unhappy animal! We'll convert him! He'll be the most converted Toad that ever was before we've done with him!"

They reached the carriage-drive of Toad Hall to find, as the Badger had anticipated, a shiny new motor-car, of great size,

painted a bright red (Toad's favourite colour), standing in front of the house. As they neared the door it was flung open, and Mr Toad, arrayed in goggles, cap, gaiters, and enormous overcoat, came swaggering down the steps, drawing on his gauntlets.

"Hullo! come on, you fellows!" he cried cheerfully on catching sight of them. "You're just in time to come with me for a jolly—to come for a jolly—for a—er—jolly—"

His hearty accents faltered and fell away as he noticed the stern unbending look on the countenances of his silent friends, and his invitation remained unfinished.

The Badger strode up the steps. "Take him inside," he said sternly to his companions.

"Now, then!" he said to the Toad, when the four of them stood together in the hall, "first of all, take those ridiculous things off!"

"Shan't!" replied Toad, with great spirit. "What is the meaning of this gross outrage? I demand an instant explanation."

"Take them off him, then, you two," ordered the Badger.

They had to lay Toad out on the floor, kicking and calling all sorts of names, before they could get to work properly. Then the Rat sat on him, and the Mole got his motor-clothes off him bit by bit, and they stood him up on his legs again.

"You knew it must come to this, sooner or later, Toad," the Badger explained severely. "You will come with me into the smoking-room, and there you will hear some facts about yourself; and we'll see whether you come out of that room the same Toad that you went in."

He took Toad firmly by the arm, led him into the smoking-room, and closed the door behind them.

"*That's* no good!" said the Rat contemptuously. "*Talking* to Toad'll never cure him. He'll *say* anything."

They made themselves comfortable in arm-chairs and waited.

After some three-quarters of an hour the door opened, and the Badger reappeared, solemnly leading by the paw a very limp and dejected Toad. His skin hung baggily about him, his legs wobbled, and his cheeks were furrowed by the tears so plentifully called forth by the Badger's moving discourse.

"Sit down there, Toad," said the Badger kindly, pointing to a chair. "Toad, I want you solemnly to repeat, before your friends here, what you fully admitted to me in the smoking-room just now. First, you are sorry for what you've done, and you see the folly of it all?"

There was a long, long pause. Toad looked desperately this way and that, while the other animals waited in grave silence. At last he spoke.

"No!" he said a little sullenly, but stoutly; "I'm *not* sorry. And it wasn't folly at all! It was simply glorious!"

"Then you don't promise," said the Badger, "never to touch a motor-car again?"

"Certainly not!" replied Toad emphatically. "On the contrary, I faithfully promise that the very first motor-car I see, poop-poop! off I go in it!"

"Very well, then," said the Badger firmly, rising to his feet. "Since you won't yield to persuasion, we'll try what force can do. Take him upstairs, you two, and lock him up in his bedroom, while we arrange matters between ourselves."

They turned the key on him and descended the stair, Toad shouting abuse at them through the keyhole; and the three friends then met in conference on the situation.

"It's going to be a tedious business," said the Badger, sighing. "I've never seen Toad so determined. However, we will see it out. He must never be left an instant unguarded. We shall have to take it in turns to be with him, till the poison has worked itself out of his system."

They arranged watches accordingly. Each animal took it in turns to sleep in Toad's room at night, and they divided the day up between them.

One fine morning the Rat, whose turn it was to go on duty, went upstairs to relieve Badger, whom he found fidgeting to be off and stretch his legs in a long ramble round his wood and down his earths and burrows. "Toad's still in bed," he told the Rat, outside the door. "Now, you look out, Rat! When Toad's quiet and submissive he's at his artfullest. There's sure to be something up. I know him. Well, now I must be off."

"How are you today, old chap?" inquired the Rat cheerfully, as he approached Toad's bedside.

He had to wait some minutes for an answer. At last a feeble voice replied, "Thank you so much, dear Ratty! So good of you to inquire! But first tell me how you are, and the excellent Mole?"

"O, *we're* all right," replied the Rat. "Mole," he added

incautiously, "is going out for a run round with Badger. They'll be out till luncheon-time, so you and I will spend a pleasant morning together, and I'll do my best to amuse you. Now jump up, there's a good fellow, and don't lie moping there on a fine morning like this!"

"Dear, kind Rat," murmured Toad, "step round to the village as quickly as possible—even now it may be too late—and fetch the doctor. And, by the way—while you are about it—I *hate* to give you additional trouble, but I happen to remember that you will pass the door—would you mind at the same time asking the lawyer to step up?"

"A lawyer! O, he must be really bad!" the affrighted Rat said to himself, as he hurried from the room, not forgetting, however, to lock the door carefully behind him. Then he ran off to the village on his errand of mercy.

The Toad, who had hopped lightly out of bed as soon as he heard the key turned in the lock, watched him eagerly from the window till he disappeared down the carriage-drive. Then, laughing heartily, he dressed as quickly as possible in the smartest suit he could lay hands on at the moment, filled his pockets with cash which he took from a small drawer in the dressing-table, and next, knotting the sheets from his bed together and tying one end of the improvised rope round the central mullion of the handsome Tudor window which formed such a feature of his bedroom, he scrambled out, slid lightly to the ground, and, taking the opposite direction to the Rat, marched off lightheartedly, whistling merrily.

"Smart piece of work that!" he remarked to himself, chuckling. "Brain against brute force—and brain came out on the top—as it's bound to do. Poor old Ratty! I must take him in hand some day, and see if I can make something of him."

Filled full of conceited thoughts such as these he strode along, his head in the air, till he reached a little inn, where he ordered the best luncheon that could be provided at so short a notice, and sat down to eat it in the coffee-room.

He was about half-way through his meal when an only too familiar sound, approaching down the street, made him start and fall a-trembling all over. The poop-poop! drew nearer and nearer, the car could be heard to turn into the inn-yard and come to a stop, and Toad had to hold on to the leg of the table to conceal his overmastering emotion. Presently the party entered the coffee-room. Toad slipped out of the room quietly, paid his bill at the bar, and sauntered round quietly to the inn-yard.

The car stood in the middle of the yard, quite unattended, the stable-helps and other hangers-on being all at their dinner.

"I wonder," Toad said to himself presently, "I wonder if this sort of car *starts* easily?"

As if in a dream he found himself, somehow, seated in the driver's seat; as if in a dream, he pulled the lever and swung the car round in the yard and out through the archway.

He was only conscious that he was Toad once more, Toad at his best and highest; the miles were eaten up under him as he sped he knew not whither, fulfilling his instincts, living his hour, reckless of what might come to him.

"To my mind," observed the Chairman of the Bench of Magistrates cheerfully, "the *only* difficulty that presents itself in this otherwise very clear case is, how we can possibly make it sufficiently hot for the incorrigible rogue and hardened ruffian whom we see cowering in the dock before us. Let me see: he has been found guilty, on the clearest evidence, first, of stealing a valuable motor-car; secondly, of driving to the public danger. It's going to be twenty years this time!"

Then Toad was loaded with chains, and dragged from the Court House, till they reached the door of the grimmest dungeon that lay in the heart of the innermost keep.

The rusty key creaked in the lock, the great door clanged behind him; and Toad was a helpless prisoner in the remotest dungeon of the best-guarded keep of the stoutest castle in all the length and breadth of Merry England.

# Toad's Adventures

Now the gaoler had a daughter, a pleasant wench and good-hearted, who assisted her father in the lighter duties of his post. Toad had many interesting talks with her, as the dreary days went on; and the gaoler's daughter grew very sorry for Toad, and thought it a great shame that a poor little animal should be locked up in prison for what seemed to her a very trivial offence.

One morning the girl was very thoughtful.

"Toad," she said presently, "just listen, please. I have an aunt who is a washerwoman."

"There, there," said Toad graciously and affably, "never mind; think no more about it. *I* have several aunts who *ought* to be washerwomen."

"Do be quiet a minute, Toad," said the girl. "As I said, I have an aunt who is a washerwoman; she does the washing for all the prisoners in this castle. You could come to some arrangement by which she would let you have her dress and bonnet and so on, and you could escape as the official washerwoman."

"Look here!" said Toad, "You wouldn't surely have Mr Toad, of Toad Hall, going about disguised as a washerwoman!"

"Then you can stop here as a toad," replied the girl with much spirit. "I suppose you want to go off in a coach-and-four!"

Honest Toad was always ready to admit himself in the wrong. "You are a good, kind, clever girl," he said, "and I am indeed a proud and stupid toad. Introduce me to your worthy aunt, if you will be so kind, and I have no doubt that the excellent lady and I will be able to arrange terms satisfactory to both parties."

Next evening the girl ushered her aunt into Toad's cell, bearing his week's washing pinned up in a towel. The old lady had been prepared beforehand for the interview, and the sight of certain golden sovereigns that Toad had thoughtfully placed on the table in full view practically completed the matter and left little further to discuss. In return for his cash, Toad received a cotton print gown, an apron, a shawl, and a rusty black bonnet. With a quaking heart, but as firm a footstep as he could command, Toad set forth.

He made his way to the station accordingly, consulted a time-table, and found that a train, bound more or less in the direction of his home, was due to start in half an hour. "More luck!" said Toad, his spirits rising rapidly, and went off to the booking-office to buy his ticket.

To his horror he recollected that he had left both coat and waistcoat behind him in his cell, and with them his pocket-book, money, keys, watch, matches, and pencil-case!

Baffled and full of despair, he wandered blindly down the platform where the train was standing and tears trickled down each side of his nose.

"Hullo, mother!" said the engine-driver, "what's the trouble? You don't look particularly cheerful."

"Oh, sir!" said Toad, crying afresh, "I am a poor unhappy washerwoman, and I've lost all my money, and can't pay for a ticket, and I *must* get home tonight somehow, and whatever I am to do I don't know. O dear, O dear!"

"Well, I'll tell you what I'll do," said the good engine-driver.

"You're a washerwoman to your trade, says you. If you'll wash a few shirts for me when you get home, and send 'em along, I'll give you a ride on my engine. It's against the Company's regulations, but we're not so very particular in these out-of-the-way parts."

They had covered many and many a mile, and Toad was already considering what he would have for supper as soon as he got home, when he noticed that the engine-driver, with a puzzled expression on his face, was leaning over the side of the engine and listening hard. Then he saw him climb on to the coals and gaze out over the top of the train; then he returned and said to Toad: 'It's very strange; we're the last train running in this direction tonight, yet I could be sworn that I heard another following us!"

Presently he called out, "I can see it clearly now! It is an engine, on our rails, coming along at a great pace! It looks as if we were being pursued!"

Then Toad fell on his knees among the coals and, raising his clasped paws in supplication, cried, "Save me, only save me, dear

kind Mr Engine-driver, and I will confess everything! I am not
the simple washerwoman I seem to be! I am a toad—the well-
known and popular Mr Toad, a landed proprietor; I have just
escaped, by my great daring and cleverness, from a loathsome
dungeon into which my enemies had flung me!''

The driver shut off steam and put on brakes, and as the train
slowed down to almost a walking pace he called out to Toad,
''Now, jump!''

Toad jumped, rolled down a short embankment, picked himself
up unhurt, scrambled into the wood and hid.

At last, cold, hungry, and tired out, he sought the shelter of a
hollow tree, where with branches and dead leaves he made
himself a bed as he could, and slept soundly till morning.

He had the world to himself, that early summer morning. Not knowing which way he ought to go, he chose to follow a canal nearby. Round a bend in the canal came plodding a solitary horse, stooping forward as if in anxious thought.

With a pleasant swirl of quiet water at its blunt bow the barge slid up alongside of him, its gaily painted gunwale level with the towing-path, its sole occupant a big stout woman wearing a linen sun-bonnet, one brawny arm laid along the tiller.

"A nice morning, ma'am!" she remarked to Toad, as she drew up level with him.

"I dare say it is, ma'am!" responded Toad politely, as he walked along the tow-path abreast of her. "I dare say it *is* a nice morning to them that's not in sore trouble, like what I am. Here's my married daughter, she sends off to me post-haste to come to her at

once; so off I comes, not knowing what may be happening or going to happen, but fearing the worst, as you will understand, ma'am, if you're a mother, too. And I've left my business to look after itself—I'm in the washing and laundering line."

"Where might your married daughter be living, ma'am?" asked the barge-woman.

"She lives near to the river, ma'am," replied Toad. "Close to a fine house called Toad Hall, that's somewheres hereabouts in these parts. Perhaps you may have heard of it."

"Toad Hall? Why, I'm going that way myself," replied the barge-woman. You come along in the barge with me."

She steered the barge close to the bank, and Toad, with many humble and grateful acknowledgements, stepped lightly on board and sat down with great satisfaction.

"What a bit of luck, meeting you!" observed the barge-woman thoughtfully. "A regular piece of good fortune for both of us. There's a heap of things of mine that you'll find in a corner of the cabin. If you'll just take one or two of the most necessary sort—I won't venture to describe them to a lady like you, but you'll recognize 'em at a glance—and put them through the wash-tub as we go along, why, it'll be a real help to me. You'll find a tub handy, and soap, and a kettle on the stove, and a bucket to haul up water from the canal with. Then I shall know you're enjoying yourself, instead of sitting here idle, looking at the scenery and yawning your head off."

Toad was fairly cornered. He fetched tub, soap, and other necessaries from the cabin, selected a few garments at random, tried to recollect what he had seen in casual glances through laundry windows, and set to.

A burst of laughter made him straighten himself and look round. The barge-woman was leaning back and laughing unrestrainedly, till the tears ran down her cheeks.

"I've been watching you all the time," she gasped. "Pretty washerwoman you are! Never washed so much as a dish-clout in your life, I'll lay!"

Toad's temper, which had been simmering viciously for some time, now fairly boiled over, and he lost all control of himself.

"You common, low, *fat* barge-woman!" he shouted; "don't you dare to talk to your betters like that! Washer-woman indeed! I would have you to know that I am a Toad, a very well-known, respected, distinguished Toad! I may be under a bit of a cloud at present, but I will *not* be laughed at by a barge-woman!"

The woman moved nearer to him and peered under his bonnet keenly and closely. "Why, so you are!" she cried. "Well, I never! a horrid, nasty, crawly Toad! And in my nice clean barge, too! Now that is a thing that I will *not* have."

She relinquished the tiller for a moment. One big mottled arm shot out and caught Toad by a fore-leg, while the other gripped him fast by a hind-leg. Then the world turned suddenly upside down, the barge seemed to flit lightly across the sky, the wind whistled in his ears, and Toad found himself flying through the air, revolving rapidly as he went.

The water, when he eventually reached it with a loud splash, proved quite cold enough for his taste, though its chill was not sufficient to quell his proud spirit.

He struck out for the shore, and, gathering his wet skirts well over his arms, he set forth on his travels again. The sun was shining brightly, and his wet clothes were soon quite dry again.

After some miles of country lanes he reached the high road, and as he turned into it, he saw approaching him something familiar.

He stepped confidently out into the road to hail the motor-car, when suddenly he became very pale, his heart turned to water, his knees shook and yielded under him, for the approaching car was the one he had stolen out of the yard of the Red Lion Hotel.

He sank down in a shabby, miserable heap in the road, murmuring to himself in his despair, "It's all up! It's all over!"

The terrible motor-car drew slowly nearer and nearer, till at last he heard it stop just short of him. Two gentlemen got out and one of them said, "O dear! this is very sad! Here is a poor old washerwoman who has fainted in the road!"

They tenderly lifted Toad into the motor-car and propped him up with soft cushions, and proceeded on their way.

When Toad heard them talk in so kind and sympathetic a way, and knew that he was not recognised, his courage began to revive, and he cautiously opened first one eye and then the other.

"Please, Sir," he said, "I wish you would kindly let me try and drive the car for a little. I've been watching you carefully, and it looks so easy."

"Bravo, ma'am! I like your spirit," said the gentleman.

Toad eagerly scrambled into the seat and set the car in motion, but very slowly at first, for he was determined to be prudent.

The gentlemen behind clapped their hands and applauded, and Toad heard them saying, "How well she does it! Fancy a washerwoman driving a car as well as that, the first time!"

This annoyed him, and he began to lose his head.

"Washerwoman, indeed!" he shouted recklessly. "Ho! ho! I am the Toad, the motor-car snatcher, the prison-breaker, the Toad who always escapes!"

With a cry of horror the whole party rose and flung themselves on him. With a half-turn of the wheel the Toad sent the car crashing through the low hedge that ran along the roadside. One

mighty bound, a violent shock, and the wheels of the car were
churning up the thick mud of a horse-pond.

Toad found himself flying through the air with the strong
upward rush and delicate curve of a swallow. He landed on his
back with a thump, in the soft rich grass of a meadow. Sitting up,
he could just see the motor-car in the pond, nearly submerged;
the gentlemen and the driver, encumbered by their long coats,
were floundering helpless in the water.

He picked himself up rapidly, and set off running across country as hard as he could, scrambling through hedges, jumping ditches, pounding across fields, ceasing to heed where he was going.

Suddenly the earth failed under his feet, he grasped at the air, and, splash! he found himself head over ears in deep water. In his blind panic he had run straight into the river!

He rose to the surface and tried to grasp the reeds and the rushes that grew along the water's edge close under the bank, but the stream was so strong that it tore them out of his hands.

Presently he saw that he was approaching a big dark hole in the bank, just above his head, and as the stream bore him past he reached up with a paw and caught hold of the edge and held on.

As he stared before him into the dark hole, some bright small thing shone and twinkled in its depths, moving towards him.

It was the Water Rat!

# The Secret Passage

The Rat put out a neat little brown paw, gripped Toad firmly by the scruff of the neck, and gave a great hoist and a pull; and the water-logged Toad came up slowly but surely over the edge of the hole, till at last he stood safe and sound in the hall.

"O Ratty!" he cried. "I've been through such times since I saw you last, you can't think! Humbugged everybody—made 'em all do exactly what I wanted! O, I *am* a smart Toad, and no mistake! What do you think my last exploit was? Wait till I tell you—"

"Toad," said the Water Rat, gravely and firmly, "you go off upstairs at once, and take off that old cotton rag that looks as if it might formerly have belonged to some washer-woman, and clean yourself thoroughly, and put on some of my clothes. Now, stop swaggering and be off! I'll have something to say to you later!"

By the time he came down again luncheon was on the table, and very glad Toad was to see it. While they ate Toad told the Rat all his adventures. As they finished their pudding Toad announced: "We'll have our coffee, and then I'm going to stroll gently down to Toad Hall, and get into clothes of my own, and set things going again on the old lines."

"Stroll gently down to Toad Hall?" cried the Rat, greatly excited. "What are you talking about? Do you mean to say you haven't heard about the Stoats and Weasels?"

"What, the Wild Wooders?" cried Toad, trembling in every limb. "No, not a word! What have they been doing?"

"—And how they've taken Toad Hall?" continued the Rat.

"O, have they!" said Toad, getting up and seizing a stick. "I'll jolly soon see about that!"

"It's no good, Toad!" cried the Rat. "You'd better come back and sit down; you'll only get into trouble. We can do nothing until we have seen the Mole and the Badger, and heard their latest news, and held conference and taken their advice in this difficult matter."

"O, ah, yes, of course, the Mole and the Badger," said Toad lightly. "What's become of them, the dear fellows? I had forgotten all about them."

"Well may you ask!" said the Rat reproachfully. "While you were riding about the country in expensive motor-cars, those two poor devoted animals have been camping out in the open, in every sort of weather, watching over your house and contriving how to get your property back for you."

Just then there came a heavy knock at the door. The Rat went straight up to the door and opened it, and in walked Mr Badger.

He came solemnly up to Toad, shook him by the paw, and said, "Welcome home, Toad! Alas! what am I saying? Home, indeed! This is a poor home-coming. Unhappy Toad!" Then he turned his back on him, sat down to the table, drew his chair up, and helped himself to a large slice of cold pie.

Presently there came another and a lighter knock. The Rat, with a nod to Toad, went to the door and ushered in the Mole, very shabby and unwashed, with bits of straw sticking in his fur.

"Hooray! Here's old Toad!" cried the Mole, his face beaming. Why, you must have managed to escape, you clever, ingenious, intelligent Toad!"

The Rat, alarmed, pulled him by the elbow; but it was too late.

Toad was puffing and swelling already.

"Clever? O now!" he said. "I'm not really clever, according to my friends. I'll tell you one or two of my little adventures, Mole, and you shall judge for yourself!"

"Toad, do be quiet, please!" said the Rat. "And don't you egg him on, Mole, when you know what he is; but please tell us as soon as possible what the position is, and what's best to be done, now that Toad is back at last."

But it was the Badger, who spoke next. "Toad!" he said severely. "You bad, troublesome little animal! Aren't you ashamed of yourself? What do you think your father, my old friend, would have said if he had been here tonight, and had known of all your goings-on?"

Toad, who was on the sofa by this time, with his legs up, rolled over on his face, shaken by sobs of contrition.

"Come, cheer up, Toady!" said the Badger. I haven't said my last word yet. Now I'm going to tell you a great secret."

Toad sat up slowly and dried his eyes.

"There—is—an—underground—passage," said the Badger impressively, "that leads from the river bank quite near here, right up into the middle of Toad Hall."

"O, nonsense! Badger," said Toad rather airily. "I know every inch of Toad Hall, inside and out. Nothing of the sort, I do assure you!"

"My young friend," said the Badger with great severity, "your father, who was a worthy animal, discovered that passage. 'Don't

let my son know about it,' he said. 'He's a good boy, but very light and volatile in character, and simply cannot hold his tongue. If he's ever in a real fix, and it would be of use to him, you may tell him about the secret passage; but not before.'"

The other animals looked hard at Toad to see how he would take it. Toad was inclined to be sulky at first; but he brightened up immediately, like the good fellow he was.

"I've found out a thing or two lately," continued the Badger.

"There's going to be a banquet tomorrow night. It's somebody's birthday—the Chief Weasel's, I believe—and all the weasels will be gathered together in the dining-hall, eating and drinking and laughing and carrying on, suspecting nothing. And that is where the passage comes in. That very useful tunnel leads right up under the butler's pantry, next to the dining-hall!"

"Aha! that squeaky board in the butler's pantry!" said Toad. "Now I understand it!"

"We shall creep out into the butler's pantry—" cried the Mole.

"—with our pistols and swords and sticks—" shouted the Rat.

"—and rush in upon them," said the Badger.

"—and whack 'em, and whack 'em, and whack 'em!" cried the Toad in ecstasy, running round and round the room, and jumping over the chairs.

"Very well, then," said the Badger, resuming his usual dry manner, "our plan is settled, and there's nothing more for you to argue and squabble about. So, as it's getting very late, all of you go right off to bed at once. We will make all the necessary arrangements in the course of the morning tomorrow."

# The Return of Toad

The following evening, when all was quite ready, the Badger took a dark lantern in one paw, grasped his great stick with the other, and said, "Now then, follow me! Mole first, 'cos I'm very pleased with him; Rat next; Toad last. And look here, Toady! Don't you chatter so much as usual, or you'll be sent back, as sure as fate!"

So at last they were in the secret passage, and the expedition had really begun! They groped and shuffled along, with their ears pricked up and their paws on their pistols, till at last the Badger said, "We ought by now to be pretty nearly under the Hall."

Then suddenly they heard, far away as it might be, and yet apparently nearly over their heads, a confused murmur of sound, as if people were shouting and cheering and stamping on the floor and hammering on tables. The Toad's nervous terrors all returned, but the Badger only remarked placidly, "They *are* going it, the weasels!"

The passage now began to slope upwards; they groped onward a little further, and they found themselves standing under the trap-door that led up into the butler's pantry.

Such a tremendous noise was going on in the banqueting-hall that there was little danger of their being overheard. The Badger said, "Now, boys, all together!" and the four of them put their shoulders to the trap-door and heaved it back. Hoisting each other up, they found themselves standing in the pantry, with only a door between them and the banqueting-hall, where their unconscious enemies were carousing.

The Badger drew himself up, took a firm grip of his stick with both paws, glanced round at his comrades, and cried:

"The hour is come! Follow me!"

And flung the door open wide.

My!

What a squealing and a squeaking and a screeching filled the air!

Well might the terrified weasels dive under the tables and spring madly up at the windows! Well might the ferrets rush wildly for the fireplace and get hopelessly jammed in the chimney! Well might tables and chairs be upset, and glass and china be sent crashing on the floor, in the panic of that terrible moment when the four Heroes strode wrathfully into the room!

They were but four in all, but to the panic-stricken weasels the hall seemed full of monstrous animals, grey, black, brown, and yellow, whooping and flourishing enormous cudgels; and they broke and fled with squeals of terror and dismay, this way and that, through the windows, up the chimney, anywhere to get out of reach of those terrible sticks.

The affair was soon over. Up and down, the whole length of the hall, strode the four Friends, whacking with their sticks at every head that showed itself; and in five minutes the room was cleared. Through the broken windows the shrieks of terrified weasels escaping across the lawn were borne faintly to their ears; on the floor lay prostrate some dozen or so of the enemy, on whom the Mole was busily engaged in fitting handcuffs. The Badger, resting from his labours, leant on his stick and wiped his honest brow.

"Mole," he said, "you're the best of fellows! Stir your stumps, Toad, and look lively! We've got your house back for you, and you don't offer us so much as a sandwich."

Toad felt rather hurt that the Badger didn't say pleasant things to him, as he had to the Mole. But he bustled about, and so did the Rat, and soon they found some guava jelly in a glass dish, and a cold chicken, a tongue that had hardly been touched, some trifle, and quite a lot of lobster salad; and in the pantry they came upon a basketful of French rolls and any quantity of cheese, butter and celery.

Then the Mole pulled his chair up to the table, and pitched into the cold tongue; and Toad, like the gentleman he was, put all his jealousy from him, and said heartily, "Thank you kindly, dear Mole, for all your pains and trouble tonight, and especially for your cleverness this morning!" The Badger was pleased at that, and said, "There spoke my brave Toad!" So they finished their supper in great joy and contentment, and presently retired to rest between clean sheets, safe in Toad's ancestral home, won back by matchless courage and a proper handling of sticks.

After this climax, the four animals continued to lead their lives, so rudely broken in upon by civil war, in great joy and contentment, undisturbed by further risings or invasions.

Sometimes, in the course of long summer evenings, the friends would take a stroll together in the Wild Wood, now successfully tamed so far as they were concerned; and it was pleasing to see how respectfully they were greeted by the inhabitants, and how the mother-weascls would bring their young ones to the mouths of their holes, and say, pointing, "Look, baby! There goes the great Mr Toad! And that's the gallant Water Rat, a terrible fighter, walking along o'him! And yonder comes the famous Mr Mole, of whom you so often have heard your father tell!"